Good MVFOL
Night!

by Julia Devanthery
illustrated by Matt Phillips

HOUGHTON MIFFLIN   BOSTON

moon

It is night. The animals are
having fun under the moon.

"It is very late," say Horse and
Frog. "How will we all get home?"

Fish

Fish says, "I will tell you how to go."

rabbit

"Rabbits and frogs can hop
home!" says Fish.
"Good night!"

bird

"Birds can fly home!" says Fish.
"Good night!"

cow

"Cows and horses can walk home!" says Fish.
"Good night!"

Snake

Fish and Snake are still here.
How will they get home?